For Alfie, who arrived one starry night, with love, Dad x

A TEMPLAR BOOK

First published in hardback in the UK in 2008 by Templar Publishing
This softback audio edition published in 2012 by Templar Publishing,
an imprint of The Templar Company Limited,
The Granary, North Street, Dorking, Surrey, RH4 1DN, UK
www.templarco.co.uk

The illustrations for this book were painted in acrylics on paper.

First softback audio edition

ISBN 978-1-84877-053-9

Edited by A. J. Wood
Designed by Mike Jolley

Printed in Hong Kong

Bob's Best ever Friend

Simon Bartram

templar publishing

It was a Tuesday morning in space
and nothing much was happening.

By ten o'clock, Bob, the **Man on the Moon**,
had finished all of his jobs for the day.

There were no space tourists to entertain and
his friends, Billy and Sam, were away on a day trip
to Pluto, visiting a most exciting pet show.
They hoped to see some alien animals there,
but Bob thought they'd be disappointed. After all,
everyone knows there's no such thing as aliens,
and especially not alien **animals**.

With nobody to talk to, Bob felt a little glum.
Then, at lunchtime, he even had to bounce on
his bouncy castle alone. And that had never,
but **never** happened before!

Quite frankly, Bob was a bit **lonely**.

To cheer himself up Bob went for a quick spin around the universe in his rocket.

Nothing much was happening there either.

Unfortunately, every last planet was closed for the winter. So Bob stopped off on a passing asteroid to enjoy a nice cup of tea and a corned beef slice. The view was beautiful. It was just a shame that he had **no one** to share it with.

"What I need," thought Bob to himself, "is a **best-ever** friend, a chum — someone to help with intergalactic missions and jigsaw puzzles — a pal who'll always be by my side."

But **where** on earth could he find a friend like that?

For the rest of the day Bob pondered his problem, until it was time to return to Earth for a nice supper of fish fingers and peas. As a Tuesday treat he allowed himself to eat in front of the TV.

The newsreader was warning that a troublesome asteroid had been causing havoc elsewhere in the solar system and was now in danger of crashing into Earth. Bob was **glued** to the screen.

He wished he had someone to watch the programme with — it was **SO** exciting.

As he sipped his cocoa in bed, Bob thought it would be so much easier if a best-ever friend could find **him** instead!

The next day Bob didn't have to start work until
the evening. So after some early star-jumps in
the garden he cycled into town to do
a spot of shopping.

Firstly, he had a quick peek around the modern
art gallery. Then he bought two smallish batteries
(to power his rocket), a smart pair of moon-patterned
underpants (half price in the sale) and a newspaper
(hot off the press).

The streets were busier than ever.
Bob wondered how on earth anyone
could hope to spot a best-ever
friend in a place
like this!

The Moon

PET SHOW PANDEMONIUM

Asteroid causes chaos by crashing into cages on planet Pluto. Escaped pets...

In the midst of his daydreams Bob suddenly found himself staring into the window of the local pet shop, 'CATS, RATS 'N' BATS'.

At first he was a trifle confused. Why had he gone there? Then he remembered Clive and Keith, his cousin Dougal's goldfish. Bob was looking after them for a day or two and that morning he thought they were looking rather peckish.

As he paid for their 'Squishy Delishy Fishy Food' (59p) a **strange** notion popped into Bob's head.

Perhaps his best-ever friend could be a **pet!!!**

Bob had a good look around inside, but he couldn't see anything that looked like a best-ever friend.

To tell you the truth, some of the animals looked a little **odd** to him.

"Oh well," sighed Bob to himself. "You can't rush these things."

His thoughts were interrupted by the chimes of the town clock. It was half past four – time for **tea!**

The best tea in town was served at the
'MOONSOUP PITSTOP CAFÉ'. Bob felt quite at home
amongst the moon pictures and decorations,
although sometimes he did call it the
'MOONSTOP PITSOUP CAFÉ' by mistake.

He wondered if anyone would recognise him
without his spacesuit on. No one did, so he sat
quietly and nibbled his favourite 'Moonsoup crater
cake'. He knew it was really just a doughnut,
but it was tip-top tasty all the same.
It was a shame there was no time
for seconds, but night was
falling and Bob had
a job to do...

The Moon was waiting!

Bob pedalled as fast as he could to the rocket launch pad and in a super-fast **flash**, changed into his man-on-the-moon suit.

He needed to reach the moon before the first 'Moon Tours' tourist spaceship arrived — there were snacks and entertainments to prepare.

After clambering aboard and flicking lots of switches, his rocket began to rumble and Bob counted down...

5... 4... 3... 2... 1... **LIFT OFF!!!**

By quarter to six he was **zooming** towards the golden moon and by six o'clock he was there.

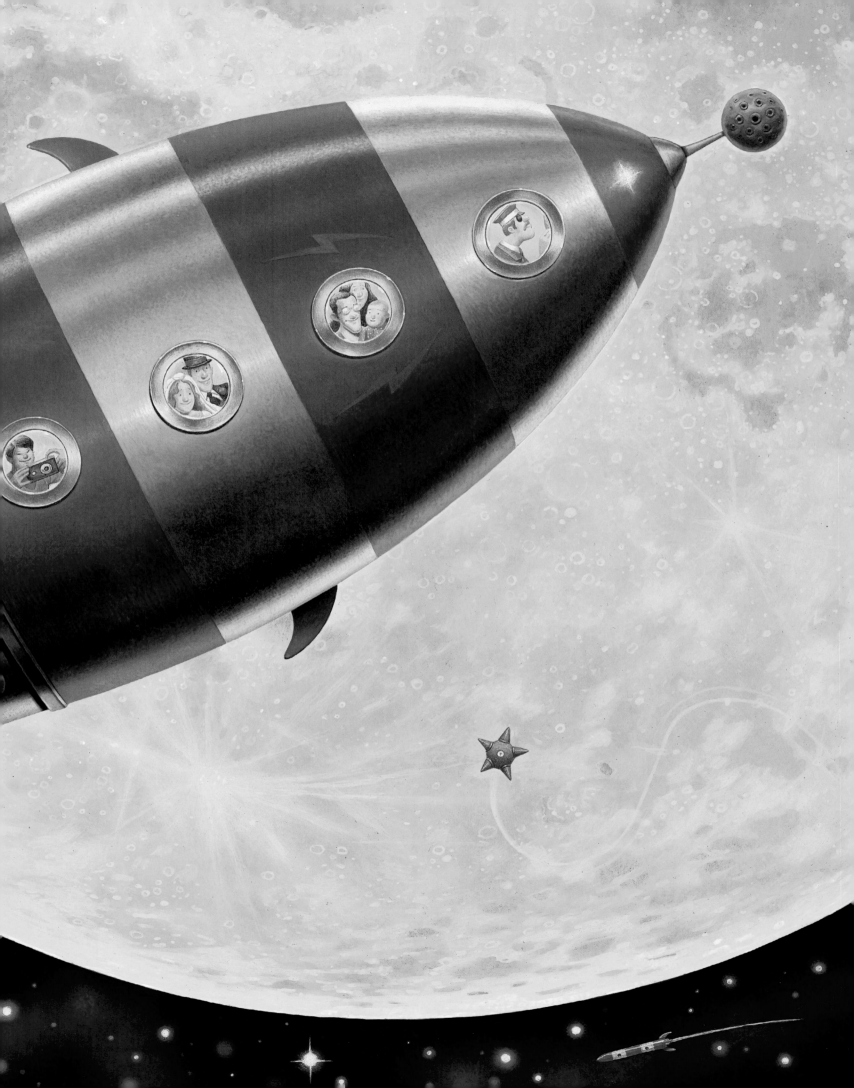

Bob welcomed the tourists with a free mini pork pie and a speech. Then he performed his thrilling moon-themed variety show and everyone went home happy.

Everyone, that is, except Bob, who was alone once more. Quietly, he packed away his props and began his weekly crater-count.

And that's when it happened!

There, popping out of crater 204, was a little furry tail. What could it be? The closer Bob got to it, the faster the tail wagged and then...
as if by magic...
something amazing shot
out of the crater.

No one in the **whole**
universe would have
expected to see what
Bob saw at that moment...

...It was a dog!!!!

The most smiley, springy dog Bob had **ever** seen.

He had no idea **where** it had come from
or **how** it had got there, but he didn't care.
He didn't even care that it looked a little odd.

All Bob knew was that from this moment onwards
they would be **best-ever friends**.

It was as if it had been written in the stars.

Bob called his dog Barry.

And each day, with their friends, they would **run** and they would **leap** and they would **play**.

Except, of course, on Tuesday lunchtimes.

On Tuesday lunchtimes...